NORTHBROOK PUBLIC LIBRARY
NORTHBROOK, IL 60062

JUN 12 2019

Northbrook Public Library

3 1123 01243 9058

W9-CEK-199

Disney · PIXAR

TOY STORY

Movie STORYBOOK

Copyright © 2019 Disney Enterprises, Inc. and Pixar. All rights reserved. MR. POTATO HEAD, MRS. POTATO HEAD, MOUSE TRAP and the
distinctive game board design, OPERATION and the distinctive game board design, PLAYSKOOL, Rockin' Robot, and TINKERTOY are trademarks
of Hasbro used with permission. © Hasbro. All rights reserved. Mattel and Fisher-Price toys used with permission. © Mattel, Inc. All rights reserved.
Pez® is a registered trademark of Pez Candy, Inc. Used with permission. All rights reserved. The Etch A Sketch® product name and configuration are
registered trademarks owned by Spin Master Ltd. Slinky Dog © POOF-Slinky, LLC. Published in the United States by Random House Children's Books,
a division of Penguin Random House LLC, 1745 Broadway, New York, NY 10019, and in Canada by Penguin Random House Canada Limited, Toronto,
in conjunction with Disney Enterprises, Inc. Random House and the colophon are registered trademarks of Penguin Random House LLC.

rhcbooks.com

ISBN 978-0-7364-4001-1

Printed in the United States of America

10 9 8 7 6 5 4 3 2 1

Disney • PIXAR
TOY STORY

Movie STORYBOOK

FEATURING

Adapted by
Bill Scollon

Illustrated by the
Disney Storybook Art Team

Andy loved playing with his toys—especially Sheriff Woody. What Andy didn't know was that his toys came to life when humans weren't around!

One morning, Woody reminded the toys that Andy and his family would be moving to a new house in a few days. "So Andy's birthday party has been moved to today," he said.

The rest of the toys groaned—they didn't like birthdays. Birthdays meant old toys could be replaced by new ones.

"They're here!" said Hamm, spotting Andy's guests when they arrived. The toys watched nervously as Andy's friends walked up the front steps.

Woody sent the Green Army Men downstairs to spy on the party. They radioed back to Andy's room on a baby monitor each time a new present was opened. When Andy was about to unwrap his final present, the baby monitor suddenly lost power. **The toys panicked.** What was the last gift?

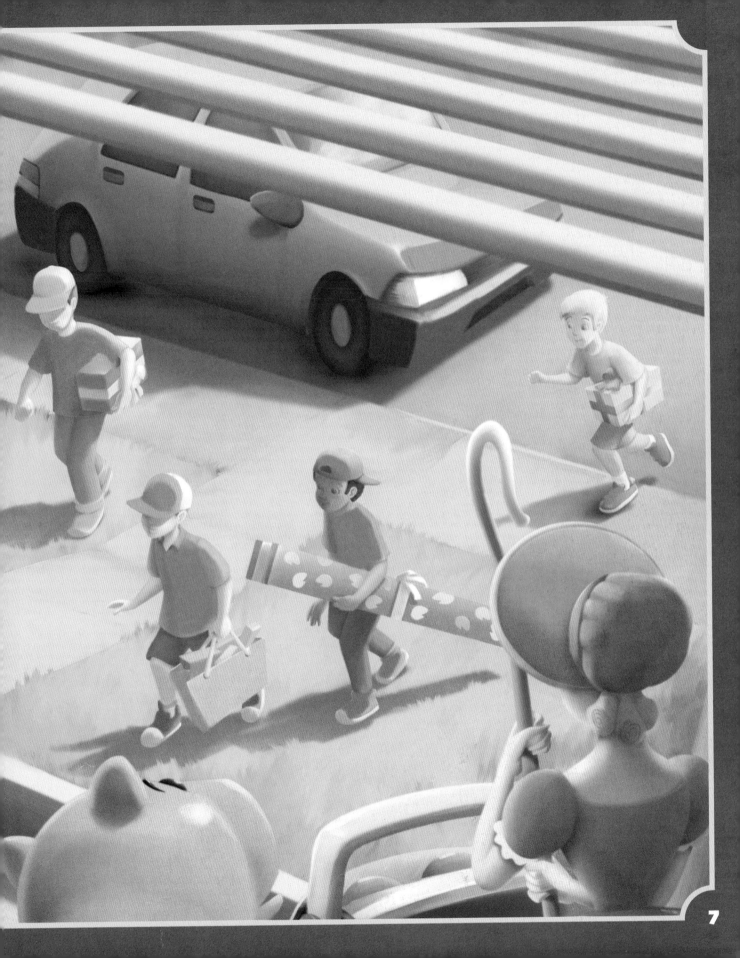

Shortly afterward, Andy burst into his bedroom and left the **mystery toy** on his bed. It was Buzz Lightyear, a space ranger who thought he had just landed on Earth! Buzz also believed he could fly. To prove it, he jumped from the bed and bounced off a ball.

"To infinity and beyond!" he shouted.

Andy's room began to **change** after Buzz arrived. Cowboy pictures were replaced by posters of **outer space**. Woody's biggest shock came one night at bedtime. When Andy climbed under the covers, he took Buzz instead of Woody!

One evening, the family went to **Pizza Planet** for dinner. Woody wanted to make sure *he* was the one to go instead of Buzz. The cowboy tried to push Buzz behind Andy's desk, but the space ranger accidentally fell out the window!

Just then, Andy came into the room, looking for Buzz. He couldn't find the space ranger anywhere! He grabbed Woody instead and ran out to the car. Moments before the car pulled away, Buzz **latched** on to the bumper!

At the restaurant, Woody saw Buzz climb into the Rocket Ship Crane Game. The space ranger thought it was a real spaceship! Woody tried to save him, but then a **huge claw** dropped down and pulled up both toys.

"All right—double prizes!" shouted the player. Woody was horrified to see it was Andy's neighbor, **Sid**. The cruel boy liked to take toys apart and rebuild them in terrifying ways.

Sid took his new toys to his bedroom, which was filled with his **strange creations**. Woody and Buzz managed to escape into the hall, where Buzz overheard a TV commercial.

"Calling Buzz Lightyear!" said the announcer. "The world's greatest superhero—now the world's greatest toy!"

Buzz was shocked. He knew he couldn't be a toy if he could fly, so he climbed onto the stairway railing and jumped. "To infinity and beyond!" he cried.

But instead of flying, he tumbled down the steps. It was true—**Buzz *was* a toy**.

Sid retrieved the escaped toys and strapped a rocket to Buzz. **Blastoff** was scheduled for the next morning.

That night, Woody explained to Buzz that being one of Andy's toys was important.

"And it's not because you're a space ranger," he said. "It's because you are *his* toy."

Buzz finally understood that Andy **needed him**.

The next morning, when Sid was about to light Buzz's rocket, he heard a strange voice. It was Woody! Suddenly, Sid's mutant toys emerged from the shadows and surrounded him.

"From now on, you must take good care of your toys. If you don't, we'll find out," said Woody, staring straight into Sid's eyes. **"So play nice!"**

Everyone cheered when Sid ran into the house. His days of torturing toys were over!

But it was moving day at Andy's house, so Woody and
Buzz raced back home. The two toys made a dash for the
moving van as it began to pull away. Woody and Buzz tried
to catch the van with help from RC, the remote-controlled car,
but RC's batteries died. Thankfully, Buzz had a rocket on his
back! Woody lit the fuse, and they **blasted into the sky**.

Just before the rocket exploded, Buzz opened his wings. "Buzz!" cried Woody. **"You're flying!"**

Woody and Buzz returned RC to the moving van and dropped through the sunroof of Andy's family car, which was just ahead. Andy was thrilled to have his favorite toys back!

Woody and Buzz were happy, too. It was good to be home.

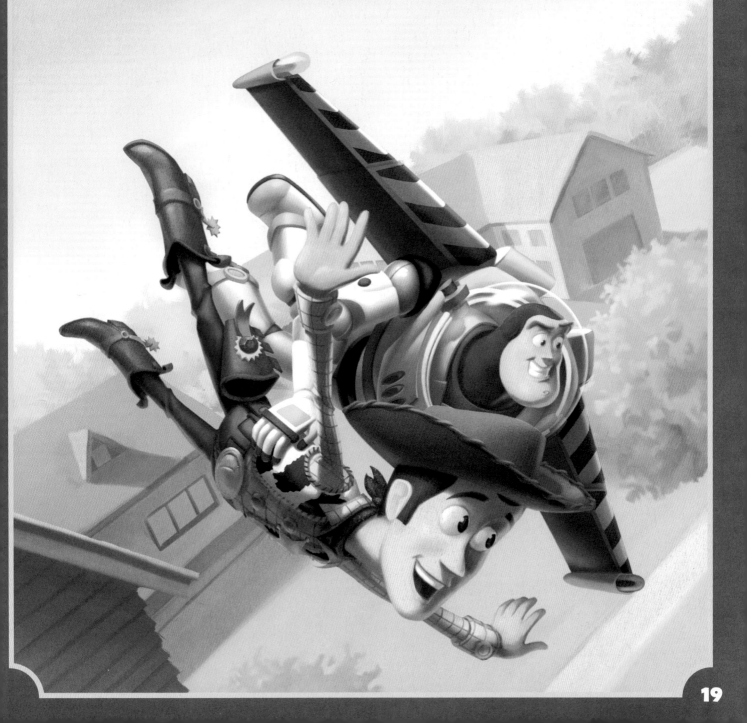

Andy's toys settled into life at the new house. While Andy played with them one last time before leaving for Cowboy Camp, Woody's shoulder tore open! Instead of going to camp with Andy, Woody would have to stay home.

Soon Andy's mom held a yard sale, and Woody tried to save a broken toy from being sold. But on his way back to the house, a toy collector nabbed the cowboy and threw him into the trunk of his car!

The collector took Woody home, repaired his torn shoulder, and placed him in a **glass box**. Then the collector put on a chicken suit.

"You, my little cowboy friend, are gonna make me big *buck-buck-bucks!*" he cackled.

As soon as the chicken man was gone, Woody tried to escape. But he was trapped!

Suddenly, two toys—a cowgirl and a horse—
jumped out of a box and ran toward Woody.
"Yee-haw!" shouted Jessie, the cowgirl.
"It's really *you!*"
Jessie introduced Woody to Bullseye, the
horse, and to the Prospector, a mint-condition
toy who had never left his box.

Woody found out that he and the other toys were characters from an old TV show called ***Woody's Roundup***. Al, the man who had taken Woody, had tons of posters, books, records, and toys from the show—but no **Sheriff Woody** until now. Al planned to sell the whole collection to a museum in Japan.

Meanwhile, Buzz and the rest of Andy's toys saw Al wearing his chicken suit in a commercial for Al's Toy Barn. Buzz led the toys on a mission to the store to **rescue** Woody.

Buzz and the other toys soon learned that Woody wasn't at the toy store, but it didn't take long for them to find him.

However, Woody **didn't want to leave**. He wanted to go to Japan with Jessie and the others because they needed him for the collection. His new friends didn't want to live in boxes anymore. Besides, what if Woody's shoulder ripped again and Andy didn't want him?

Buzz and the others sadly climbed into the air vent and left—**without Woody**.

Woody realized he had been wrong. He told Jessie and Bullseye that living in Andy's room would be better than a museum. They could leave with him!

The Prospector suddenly **slammed** the vent shut! He wasn't about to let Woody go—he knew no museum would want the collection without the cowboy.

Just then, Al appeared. He **packed all four toys** into a case and left for the airport!

Outside, Buzz and the other toys spotted Al on the way to his car. Woody was trying to escape! Buzz and the others hopped into a Pizza Planet truck and **followed** their cowboy friend.

Inside the airport, the toys spotted Al's case in the baggage-handling area. When Woody tried to escape, the Prospector popped out of his box to stop him! Woody and Bullseye were finally able to **get away**—but they still had to save Jessie!

Woody scrambled onto the plane and quickly found the cowgirl. The two friends dropped through a door that opened over the plane's wheels as the jet began to speed down the runway. Woody saw Buzz riding Bullseye beneath the plane. Using his lasso, Woody and Jessie **swung off the plane**—and landed on Bullseye. They were safe and sound!

When Andy got back from Cowboy Camp, he was happily surprised. **"New toys!"** he cried. "Thanks, Mom!" Jessie and Bullseye had proudly joined his favorite friends, and they all welcomed him home.

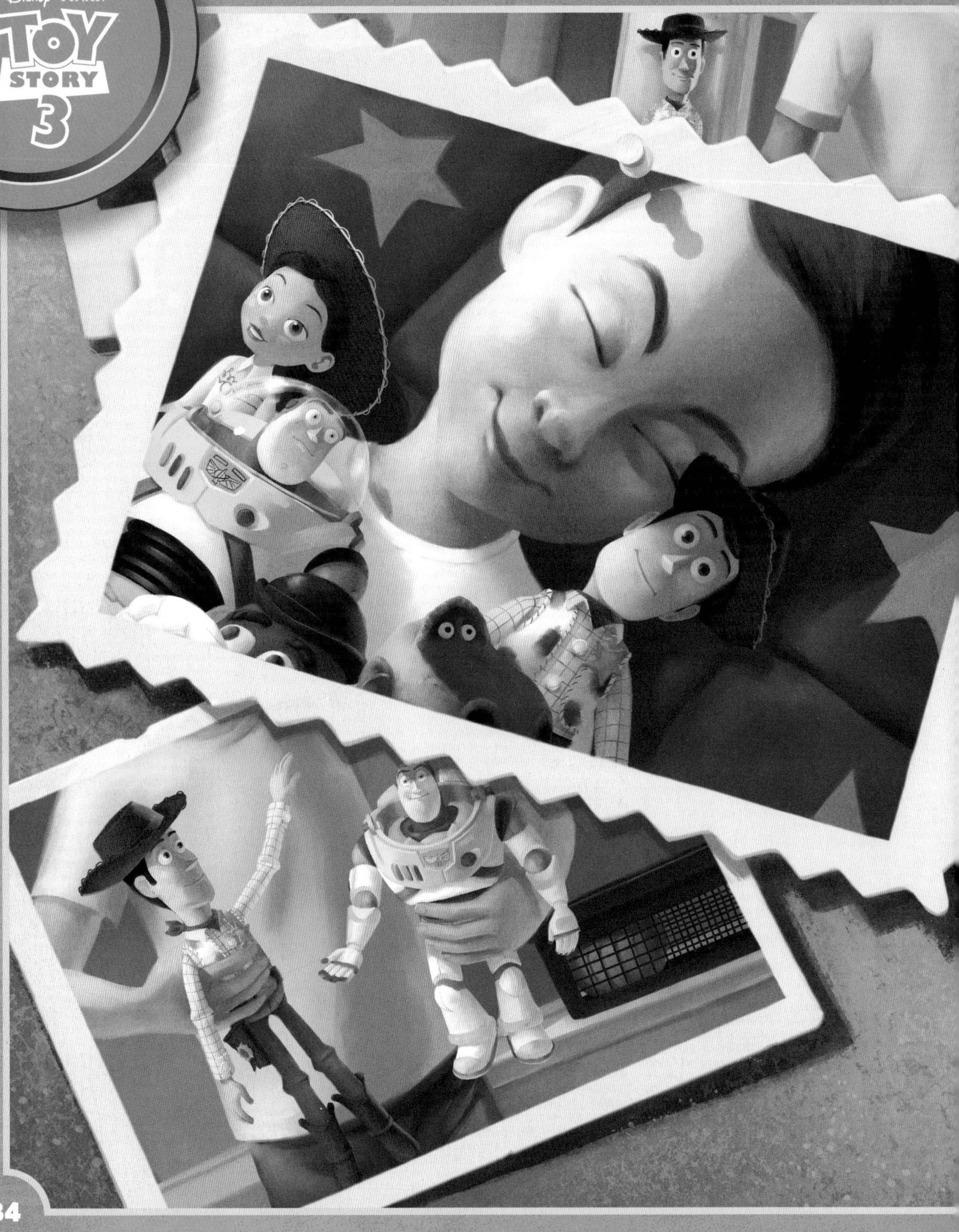

Years went by, and as Andy grew, he stopped playing with his toys. He would soon be going away to college. Woody was the only toy Andy was planning to take with him. He put the other toys in a plastic bag.

But there was a **mix-up**. Instead of being stored in the attic, the plastic bag was put outside on **garbage day**! Woody told the toys it had been an accident, but they didn't believe him. The toys hopped into a donation box headed for Sunnyside Daycare. Woody tagged along, trying to get them to return to Andy's house.

Lotso, a big pink bear, welcomed them to Sunnyside Daycare. The toys were taken to the Caterpillar Room, where the smallest kids played.

Woody still thought they should all go back to Andy's house, but everyone else **loved** Sunnyside.

Woody headed out alone. Along the way, he got **stuck in a tree**, where a little girl named **Bonnie** found him. She gently freed the cowboy, put him in her backpack, and took him to her house.

The other toys soon learned the truth about the Caterpillar Room. The toddlers there played **too rough**! Through a window, Buzz saw other kids playing nicely in the Butterfly Room.

Once school ended for the day, Buzz sneaked out to learn more about the Butterfly Room. He overheard Lotso's gang talking about Andy's toys. They'd been put in the roughest room on purpose! Just then, the space ranger was **snatched up** and taken to Lotso.

Lotso told Andy's toys that they had to **stay where they were**. Somebody had to put up with the youngest kids—and it was not going to be Lotso and his gang.

The next day, Woody went back to the daycare in Bonnie's backpack. He and the rest of the toys came up with an **escape plan**.

The toys **crept** to the toolshed on the other side of the playground. After they got inside, they jumped down a trash chute. Unfortunately, Lotso was waiting for them!

The toys tried to get past the bear, but they fell into a **dumpster**—just as a garbage truck arrived! The truck hauled all the toys to the dump.

At the dump, some toys called the Aliens spotted a crane. **"Oooh! The claaaww . . . ,"** they murmured. As they ran toward it, a bulldozer pushed the other toys onto a conveyor belt that fed into a giant shredder.

The gang avoided being shredded, but Lotso got stuck. Buzz and Woody boosted Lotso out of the pit so he could turn off the machine. Instead, the dishonest bear **ran away**.

Luckily, the Aliens returned and used the crane's **giant claw** to save everybody from certain doom!

After their escape, the toys wanted to get back to Andy's room. Compared to Sunnyside, being stored in the attic sounded pretty good!

Woody had an even better idea. He crossed out **"Attic"** and wrote **"Donate."** Then he wrote the address to Bonnie's house. Woody sneaked into the box with his friends just as Andy came through the door.

Andy had no idea who had written "Donate" on the box, but he knew it was a good idea. Giving his toys to someone who would **love them** and **play with them** was much better than leaving them in the attic.

Bonnie was delighted when Andy arrived with his box of toys. She loved every one of them, but she was especially excited to spot Woody.

"My cowboy!" she squealed.

Andy smiled. The toys smiled, too. Their time with Andy was ending, but their adventures with Bonnie were **just beginning**.

Many years ago, one of Andy's toys
was left out in the rain. Bo Peep and Woody worked
together to save the toy. But when Woody tried to get
back into the house, he was shocked to see Andy's mom
putting Bo in a box! Sadly, Andy's little sister, Molly,
didn't want Bo anymore.

Woody tried to convince Bo to stay with him and the other toys, but her mind was made up.
"It's time for the next kid," she said. Bo wanted Woody to come with her, but at that moment, he heard Andy calling for him. Woody knew he couldn't leave his kid, so the two toys said **goodbye**.

Some time later, Andy **outgrew** his toys and gave them to an imaginative little girl named Bonnie.

Bonnie took Woody, Buzz, and their friends on lots of new and **exciting adventures**.

But Woody eventually found himself being played with **less and less**.

One morning, Woody heard Bonnie's dad say it was almost time to leave for kindergarten orientation. Bonnie was **nervous**, so Woody jumped into her backpack to keep an eye on her.

The teacher asked the class to work on a craft project. While Bonnie was working, some of the art supplies at her table **spilled** into a trash can! Woody watched as Bonnie's eyes filled with tears. He climbed out of her backpack and removed the art supplies from the garbage. Woody slipped them and some other items onto the table and then jumped back into the bag.

Bonnie happily picked up a spork and glued a pair of eyes on it. Then she added arms, legs, and a few more touches. She was proud of her work—she named the spork **Forky**.

Bonnie put Forky into her backpack. To Woody's surprise, the googly-eyed art project **came to life**!

Back at home, Woody introduced a nervous Forky to Bonnie's other toys.

Woody's friends weren't sure about Forky—they had never seen a toy like him! Woody said Forky was **very important** to Bonnie right now, so they all had to protect him.

However, Forky had a habit of jumping into the trash. Woody would have to keep a close eye on him. . . .

Since kindergarten didn't start for another week, Bonnie's family decided to take a **road trip**. Woody, Forky, and the other toys were packed up and loaded into an RV.

At every stop, Forky tried to climb into the trash! Woody spent all his time chasing Forky and dragging him back to the RV. By the end of the day, Woody was **exhausted**.

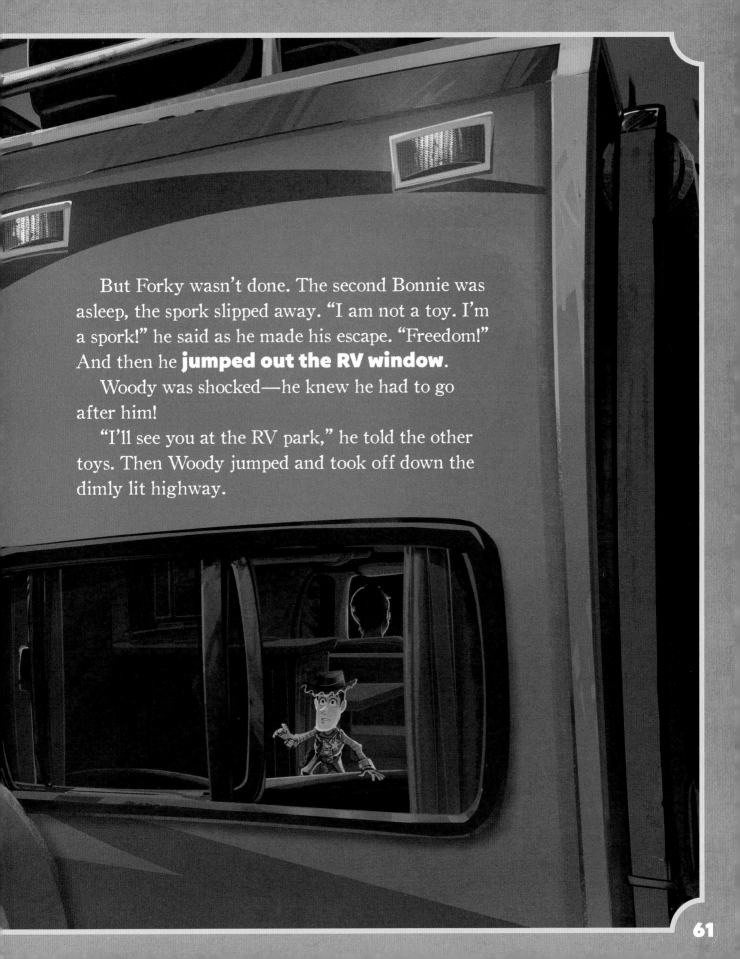

But Forky wasn't done. The second Bonnie was asleep, the spork slipped away. "I am not a toy. I'm a spork!" he said as he made his escape. "Freedom!" And then he **jumped out the RV window**.

Woody was shocked—he knew he had to go after him!

"I'll see you at the RV park," he told the other toys. Then Woody jumped and took off down the dimly lit highway.

The cowboy soon found Forky. As he dragged the spork toward the RV park, he tried to get Forky to understand how important he was to Bonnie.

"Like it or not, **you are a toy**," said Woody. "You have to be there for Bonnie." He explained that Bonnie loved Forky the same way Forky loved trash.

"I get it now," said Forky. "I'm Bonnie's trash!"

Suddenly, the spork started running. "Woody, we got to get going," he said. **"She needs me!"**

As Woody and Forky neared the RV park, they passed the Second Chance Antiques Store, where something caught Woody's eye. It was the **lamp** that had once belonged to his old friend Bo Peep!

He hadn't seen Bo in years.

Forky wanted to keep moving, but Woody needed to see if Bo was in the shop. He picked up the spork and climbed through the mail slot.

Woody found no sign of Bo or her sheep in the shop. But when Woody and Forky were leaving, they met a doll named **Gabby Gabby** and her friend Benson, a ventriloquist's dummy.

Woody explained that he was looking for Bo Peep. Gabby Gabby listened politely, but she couldn't take her eyes off his **pull string**. It looked exactly like hers. . . .

Gabby Gabby agreed to help Woody find Bo Peep. "We'll take you to her," she said.

As they went through the store, Gabby Gabby told Woody that her record was fine, but the voice box for her pull string had always been **broken**. She wondered aloud if Woody's voice box would fit her.

Woody was nervous. "We gotta go," he whispered to Forky.

"You can't leave," said Gabby Gabby. "You have what I need."

Woody and Forky were quickly **surrounded** by more of the doll's friends! Woody dashed into an aisle just as Forky was grabbed. The quick-thinking cowboy saw a little girl coming. He pulled the string on his voice box and dropped to the floor.

The store owner's granddaughter, Harmony, picked up Woody. She smiled and whisked him off to the playground. Woody had no choice but to leave Forky behind!

At the playground, Woody tried to sneak off to rescue Forky. But before he could get away, a **bus full of campers** arrived! The kids grabbed the toys and ran around the playground. Woody froze just before a girl saw him and snatched him up. She introduced Woody to another toy—amazingly, it was Bo Peep!

When the girl wasn't looking, the two friends ran for cover behind some bushes. Woody was sorry to hear that Bo didn't have a kid anymore. She was a lost toy now, but she said **she loved it**. As they caught up, Bo's skunkmobile appeared, driven by her loyal sheep, Billy, Goat, and Gruff.

Bo introduced Woody to a tiny pet detective named **Giggle McDimples**. Woody asked Bo and Giggle to help him save Forky. Bonnie needed him! But Bo and Giggle never wanted to go back to the antiques store—it had taken them years to escape that place.

Woody reminded Bo of Molly, the girl who had loved her for so many years. Finally, Bo was convinced.

In the antiques shop, Gabby Gabby had taken Forky to her cabinet and asked him to tell her everything about his friend Woody. When Harmony returned from the park, Gabby Gabby watched the little girl pull out her tea set. The doll **mimicked** every move Harmony made.

In Gabby Gabby's mind, Harmony was the **perfect little girl**. All the doll wanted was to belong to Harmony, and only one thing stood in her way.

"When my voice box is fixed, I will finally get my chance," said Gabby Gabby.

That morning, Buzz had left the RV in search of Woody and Forky, but a carnival game-booth operator found *him* instead. Buzz was immediately strapped to the prize wall of the Star Adventurer booth beside two plush toys, **Ducky and Bunny**. They were not happy that Buzz had taken their top-prize spot!

Ducky kicked at Buzz, but the space ranger closed his helmet on Ducky's foot! As the toys struggled, they all fell from the prize wall.

"Put us back up there!" demanded Bunny.

But Buzz was already on the move.

Bo led the toys through the carnival to the antiques store. On the roof, Bo and the toys met up with Buzz, who was followed closely by Ducky and Bunny. Bo and Woody explained their mission, and everyone agreed to **work together** to save Forky.

"Okay, guys. Playtime is over," said Bo, crouching by an opening on the roof of the store. "You have to follow my lead."

Back at the RV, the toys realized that Bonnie's dad was about to start driving away. They had to stop him. They couldn't leave Woody, Buzz, and Forky behind!

POP! went a tire.

"We're not going anywhere," Jessie told her friends, holding up a nail. "If you get my *point*."

Inside the store, Bo, Buzz, and Woody saw that they had to cross an open aisle to save Forky. They also had to watch out for **Dragon**, the vicious cat who lived in the shop.

Suddenly, Bonnie and her mom came in! Woody acted quickly. He started to run into the aisle, but Bo pulled him back. Benson had spotted Woody and started closing in. Thankfully, Bo's sheep took a bite out of Benson, which sent him running—**with the sheep!**

Now Gabby Gabby had the sheep *and* Forky!

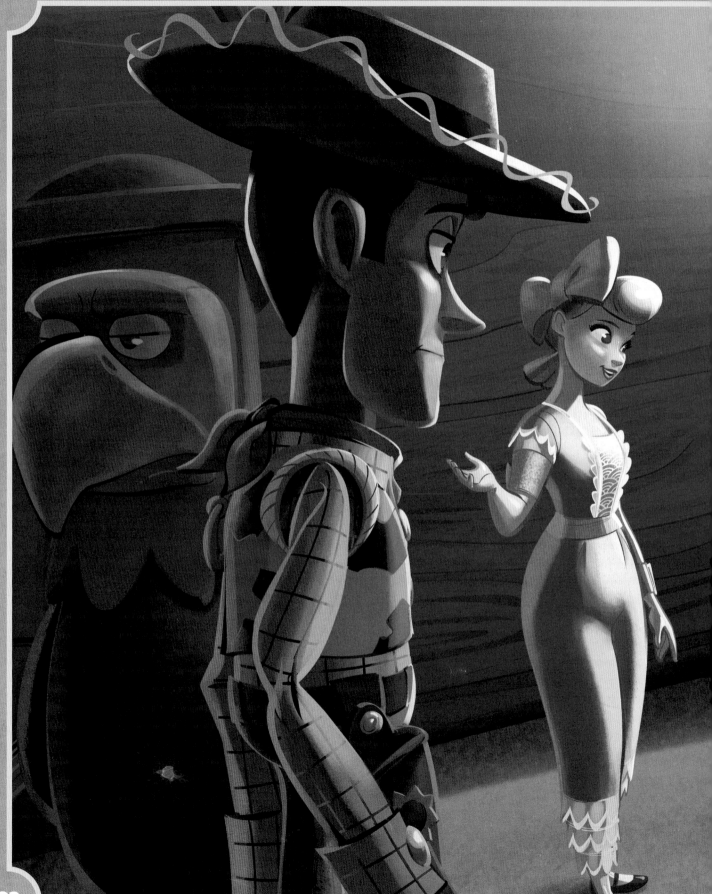

Bo had another plan. She went looking for a toy named **Duke Caboom**. He was Canada's greatest stuntman! When they found him, Bo explained that Forky and her sheep were being held by Gabby Gabby. To rescue them, she needed the daredevil to jump over the aisle to Gabby Gabby's cabinet. But Duke hadn't attempted a jump in years.

"No!" said Duke. "Nuh-uh. Negative!"

As Woody explained how important Forky was to his kid, Duke got choked up. Years before, Duke had had a kid named Rejean. But the stuntman hadn't been able to jump like the toy in the TV commercial, so Rejean **had given him away**.

"Forget your commercial," said Bo. "Be the Duke you are right now! The one who jumps and *crashes*."

Duke finally agreed to help.

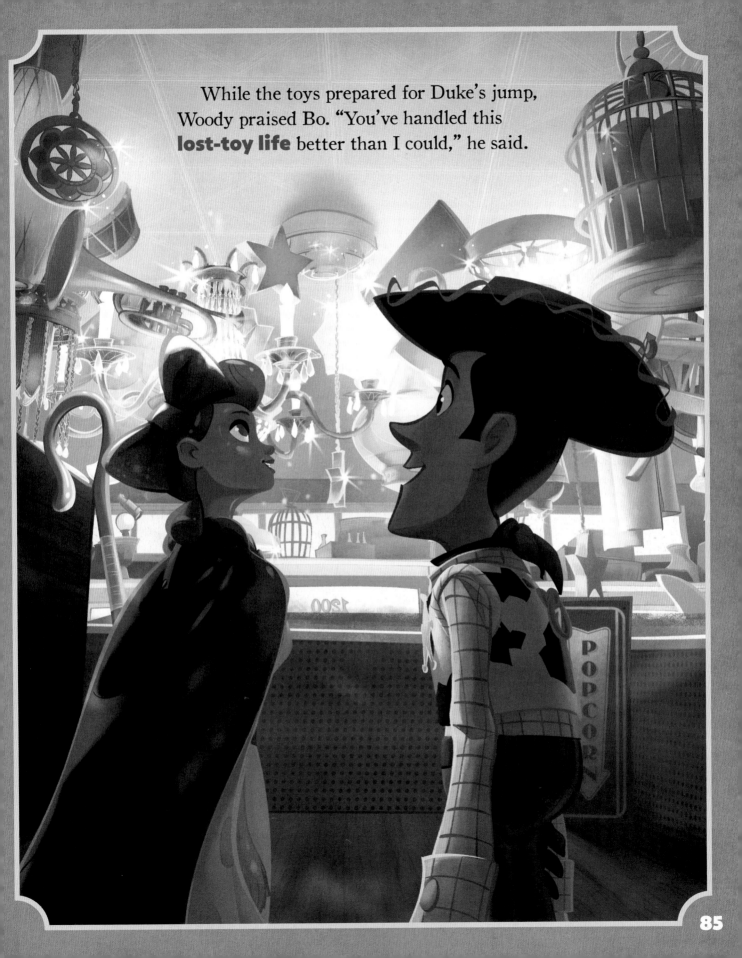

While the toys prepared for Duke's jump, Woody praised Bo. "You've handled this **lost-toy life** better than I could," he said.

Finally, the mission was under way. Woody climbed onto the motorcycle behind Duke. The stuntman sped off, but then he thought of Rejean—and lost control! Woody jumped off the bike and grabbed the cabinet just as Duke **crashed** to the floor.

Woody soon found Forky and ran. But Gabby Gabby's friends grabbed his pull string! In the mayhem, Woody lost Forky, fell off the cabinet, and landed on top of Dragon! The rest of the toys, except for Forky, grabbed the string attached to Woody.

Duke roared past Dragon on his motorcycle. The cat **chased** the daredevil through the store, **dragging** the rest of the toys outside.

Woody wanted to go back for Forky, but **no one** wanted to go with him.

"Open your eyes, Woody," said Bo. "There's plenty of kids out there. It can't be just about the one you're still clinging to."

"It's called loyalty," snapped Woody. "Something a lost toy wouldn't understand."

Bo left for the carnival, while Buzz returned to the RV. Once again, **Woody was on his own**.

When Woody went back into the antiques store, he thought he'd have to fight for Forky, but Gabby Gabby just wanted to talk.

"I was **defective** right out of the box," she said. She could only imagine how wonderful it was for Woody to have spent so much time with Andy and Bonnie.

Woody and Gabby Gabby reached an agreement. Woody would give Gabby Gabby his voice box, and in return, she would let Forky go.

Moments later, it was finally Gabby Gabby's chance. Harmony found Gabby Gabby and pulled her string. "Let's be best friends," the doll said with her new voice box. Harmony stared at Gabby Gabby, then tossed her into an old crate!

"Too creepy," she said.

Woody was shocked.

Just then, Bonnie returned to the store to get the backpack she had left there. Woody told Forky to go with Bonnie and to tell the other toys to get the RV to the carnival where he would meet them. Then the cowboy went back to help Gabby Gabby.

Woody told Gabby Gabby that Harmony wasn't her only chance at a good life—he would take her to his kid, Bonnie!

"A friend once told me there are **plenty of kids out there**," he said. "And one of them is named Bonnie. She's waiting for you right now. She just doesn't know it yet."

Just then, Bo appeared. She had returned to the store to help Woody.

Woody and Bo caught up with the rest of the toys. But they needed to find a quick way to get to the RV on the other side of the carnival. Bo and Woody convinced Duke that he could jump from the Ferris wheel to the Star Adventurer booth.

"I can do this!" he said.

"Yes, you **CAN-ada**," replied Woody.

Seconds later, Canada's greatest stuntman flew through the air and **landed** on the roof of the booth. The rest of the toys quickly followed on a zip line.

The toys raced to the carousel, but as they got close, Gabby Gabby noticed a lost girl. Woody could see how much Gabby Gabby wanted to **help** her.

"I think I can be there for her," said Gabby Gabby. "This is my chance." The toys devised a new plan to get the girl to notice the doll.

"I'm Gabby Gabby. Will you be my friend?" she said in her recorded voice.

The girl picked up Gabby Gabby and hugged her tight. "Are you lost, too?" she asked. **"I'll help you."**

Just then, a security guard came along and reunited the girl with her parents. Gabby Gabby finally got her kid!

Woody and Bo met up with Bonnie's toys at the RV. The toys were happy to see them, and Woody was even happier to see Forky with Bonnie again. He had done the job he'd set out to do. Woody realized that there were other **kids and toys** all over who needed his help. And wherever he went, he would always have **friends by his side**.